this book belongs to:

to Sylvia

This paperback edition first published in 2008 by Andersen Press Ltd.
First published in Great Britain in 2005 by Andersen Press Ltd.,
20 Vauxhall Bridge Road, London SW1V 2SA.
Published in Australia by Random House Australia Pty.,
Level 3, 100 Pacific Highway, North Sydney, NSW 2060.

Colour separated in Italy by Fotoriproduzioni, Grafiche, Verona.
Printed and bound in Singapore.

10 9 8 7 6 5 4 3 2 1

British Library Cataloguing in Publication Data available.

ISBN 978 1 84270 563 6

nutmeg

by David Lucas

Andersen Press
London

There was *always* cardboard for breakfast.

There was *always* string for lunch.

There was *always* sawdust for supper.

The living room was full of junk.
Nutmeg looked out of the window.
Cousin Nesbit fiddled with bits of things.
Uncle Nicodemus sat in his chair and dozed.

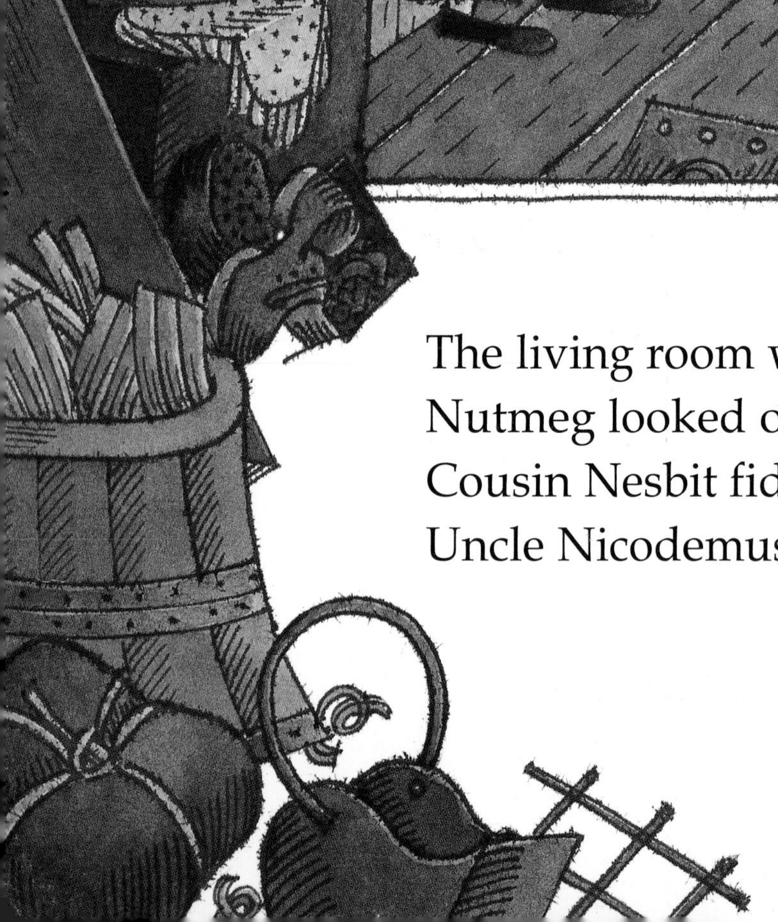

Nutmeg stood up.
"I am going for a *walk,*" she said.
"Why?" said Cousin Nesbit.
"Whatever for?" said Uncle Nicodemus.
"I don't *know*!" said Nutmeg.

But she went for a walk nevertheless.

Nutmeg walked to the Creek.
She sat and watched the tide come in.

What was that?
There was a bottle at the water's edge.

There seemed to be a tiny light inside.
Nutmeg opened the bottle.

Out burst a Genie.

"I have been trapped for a thousand years," said the Genie. "You have set me free. In return I shall grant you three wishes."
"Three wishes?" said Nutmeg.
"Yes," said the Genie. "Now come on . . . what do you want?"
"But I don't know what I want," she said.
"Of course you do. Just think!"
Nutmeg thought.
"Come on . . . *come on!*" said the Genie.
"I would very much like something *different* for supper," said Nutmeg, at last.
"And?"
". . . and something *different* for breakfast."
"And?"
". . . and something *different* for lunch."

"There!" said the Genie, and handed her a Spoon, a magic Spoon.
Then, in a flash
and a bang,
he was gone.

Nutmeg hurried home.

The Spoon conjured up all kinds of ingredients.

The Spoon cooked supper all by itself.

And that night they all went to sleep with a smile.

In the night
Nutmeg heard a noise:

Bing

BANG

Bong!

Clatter

Clatter

CRASH!

Nutmeg crept
downstairs.

The Spoon wasn't cooking.
The Spoon was stirring up the kitchen.

Bang Bang Clatter CRASH!

"Stop it!" said Nutmeg. "Stop it!"

Uncle Nicodemus hurried on to the landing.
Cousin Nesbit slid down the banister.

The Spoon stirred up the living room.

"Behave yourself, Master Spoon!"
said Uncle Nicodemus.
Cousin Nesbit shook his fist.

The Spoon stirred up the *whole* house.
"Hold tight!" said Uncle Nicodemus.

The Spoon stirred up the land and sea.
The Spoon mixed up the stars.

Nutmeg dared not look.
"Be brave now, shipmates!"
said Uncle Nicodemus. "Be brave!"

splash!

The wind was soft, the sun was rising,
and the Spoon was nowhere to be seen.

Nutmeg took the wheel.
Cousin Nesbit hoisted the flag.
"Land ho!" cried Uncle Nicodemus.

"Something different for breakfast too!"
said Nutmeg.

And after breakfast they set sail again, and it wasn't long before Nutmeg began to wonder what they'd have for *lunch*.

Look out for other books by

DAVID LUCAS

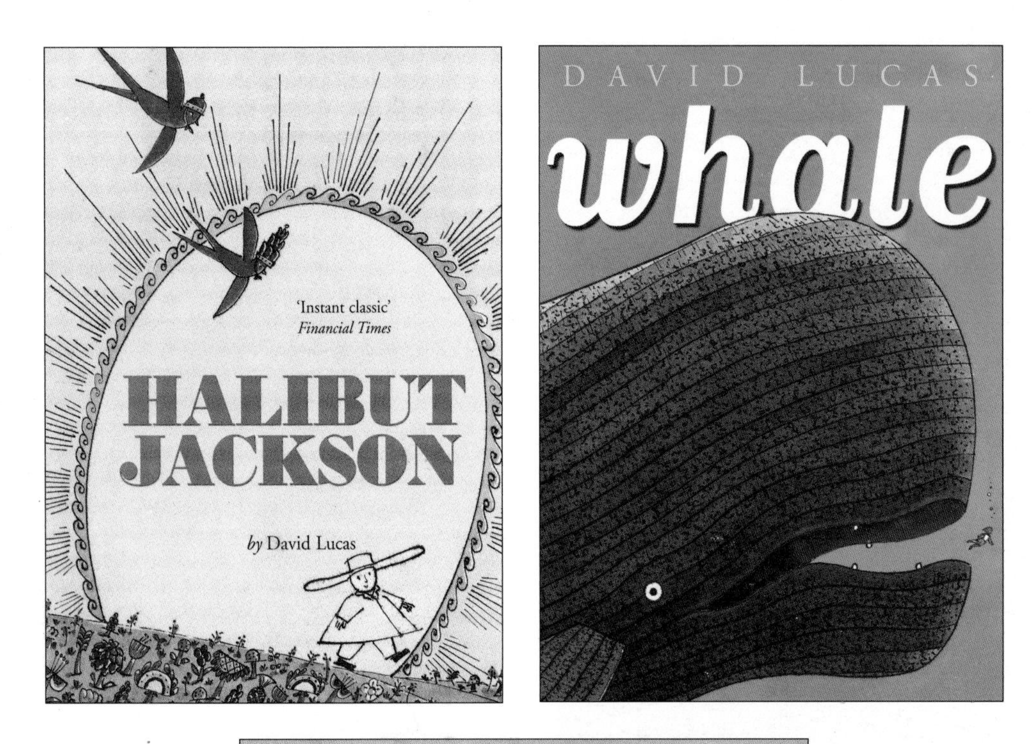